Rachel Wooley
7/6/20

Captain Hornet

Written and Illustrated by
Rachel Woolsey

Published in the United States of America by:

Cobb Publishing
www.CobbPublishing.com
Charleston, AR.

ISBN: 9781798216231

A special thanks to my dear ol' ma for
encouraging me to get this book published!

And to all those who helped me: thank you!
You made a dream come true!

Chapter 1:
An Adventure

More than anything I wanted to sail on the ocean in a grand ship, and I was doing my best to convince my grandpa that it was okay. So far…, it wasn't working.

"Why, grandpa, I don't see what's so wrong with traveling around in search of new lands?"

"Stop talking nonsense, Marlin."

"I'm not talking nonsense. I mean it."

"Marlin, it's foolish to waste your time seeking beyond what you can't see. I didn't raise you to throw your life away."

With that said, I went back to sweeping the floor. My grandpa and I lived in a small abode about a mile away from the shore. He owned a fish store that needed a lot of work. The front, dusty windows were cracked in places, and several of the floorboards needed to be re-placed. Overall it was just a tiny, musty place at the edge of the beach. I helped him around there, even though I didn't care about the place at all. I'd rather do other things than run a store. Business was slow, and life there seemed too quiet. There were so few customers that it was challenging to keep the place going. To me it was a waste of time, but grandpa claimed it was a simple, honest living.

"Don't you worry, Marlin. Things will pick up in a few months."

It wasn't like I was worried about the store, and I didn't want to get used to it. No, I had other ideas buried in the deep depths of my mind. My aim was an adventure. I aspired to explore islands and discover buried treasure or perhaps hunt down an exotic creature in a dangerous jungle and sell it, becoming rich. If only I had money, I could get grandpa out of this dump. However, I felt that these were just silly, fanciful dreams because I was convinced that my life had been planned out for me. My grandpa wanted me to inherit the shop, and that's all my life would amount to. I suppose it had to do with what happened to my parents.

"Grandpa, how did my parents die?" I asked.

"Why do you want to know? It doesn't matter how they died!"

"But I have a right to know!"

My grandpa's rather gruff and hard in his ways. I can tell it bothers him. Every time I try to talk about it, his temper flares, and his blue eyes start watering. He then turns his head away, so I won't see him cry. My parents died when I was just an infant, so I didn't even know what they looked like. I've always wondered about them. This time when I asked the question, he at last turned back around and gave me an answer.

"They died at sea," he muttered. "There was a great storm, and their ship was hit by lightning. The ship caught fire."

"How do you know this?"

"Because there were two survivors."

"Who were the survivors?"

For a moment my grandpa hesitated. He was almost afraid to answer, but he finally decided that it was time I should know. I think he realized that I was getting older. After all, I was twelve years old and not a little boy anymore.

"You and me."

"We were the survivors?"

"Yes, your parents told me to get into the boat with you. I begged them to get in with me."

"They wouldn't get in?"

"They wanted to put the fire out and save the other crew members. It was foolish of them. Now I don't want to talk about this any-more."

So, my parents were drowned at sea. No wonder grandpa hated the ocean. It then oc-curred to me that because of my parent's death, I may never get to travel the world. But I was wrong. My adventure began later that night.

My grandpa and I were about to close the shop. We were checking around to make sure all the items were stocked when grandpa slammed me to the ground.

"Stay down!" he ordered.

A huge cannon ball missed my head. It crashed through one of the front windows. The glass shattered, covering the wooden floor. I rolled over on my side to get away from the debris.

"Quick, follow me!" said grandpa.

Without argument I obeyed. Together we fled out of the store and raced inland while cannon balls were being fired at us, one ball after another crashing down onto the ground, sending up waves of dust. I coughed and gagged but kept going. I didn't dare glance back.

"Listen to me, I have to go back to the house and get some things," he said. "I want you to run toward the hills as fast as you can."

"No, I won't leave you!"

"Do as I say, boy!"

I heard shouting, and grandpa took off, vanishing behind a palm tree. I should have listened to him, but I was afraid. Instead I made the terrible mistake of waiting for his return. A dirty, filthy pirate snuck up on me. Before I comprehended what was happening, I was blindfolded and bound. The pirate spoke in my ear, but I couldn't understand what he was saying. His rotten breath hit my nostrils, causing me to gag. He had been drinking, and his words were slurring into unintelligible garble. I was then lugged away and placed into a rowboat. Shortly after, he rowed me to a pirate ship, a sloop, where I was forced to get on.

"Welcome to my ship!" The pirate exclaimed triumphantly, yanking the blindfold off.

I stood on the deck and stared at the captain. His greeting was more of a snobbish comment than a welcome, and his face was worn and rugged from the sun. He stared at me with his cold eyes, holding a pistol in his hand.

"My name is Captain Hurricane, and you are my slave!"

He said this forcefully. He wanted me to know he meant business, and I believed him. I was convinced he would kill me without any remorse.

"Do you understand? When you disobey me, you will receive lashes. There will be no mercy from me."

When he said this, the crew cheered. They loved hearing those harsh words. It was clear that they carried no high standards of moral values.

"Do you understand, boy?"

"Aye, sir."

Every limb in my body was shaking. I couldn't look him in the eye. He liked that. Captain Hurricane loved the fear he had driven into me. A moment later he sent me to work, swabbing the deck. Anger and desire for revenge filled me while I swished my dirty mop back and forth. They would pay one day, and I would be watching.

Chapter 2:
A Turn of Events

I received many beatings over the next few days, and I was bruised and aching all over from the horrible treatment. With each step I felt my muscles tighten from the work I was forced to do. Not to mention the lashes I received every now and then. It wasn't enough to kill me but just enough to make me wish that I was dead, and sometimes I wished more than anything that I was. Even death would be better than this.

Every day in my head, I planned of ways to escape, but I knew that all my schemes would fail. How could I get off the ship, and where could I go? The ocean is wide, a death sentence waiting to happen.

As I was thinking about this, something unexpected happened. A cannon ball hit the fore mast. In haste I leaped out of the way before it could hit me, and I saw Captain Hurricane and his crew sprint out from the hatch. He ordered his crew to grab muskets and load the cannons. I was handed a musket by a crew member, but I wouldn't fire it. I was afraid to. We were under attack, but I had no idea who was firing at us.

"Shoot lad!" yelled a man.

I raised my musket to fire but changed my mind. I realized that this was my chance to get off this ship before it sunk, so I pretended to fire, until I found an opportunity to escape. A second later I bounded overboard and swam out into the ocean.

I heard shouts from above and gun shots. I was being fired upon! I submerged into the water and emerged again to avoid getting shot. When I did surface again, I spotted the other ship and traveled to it. I knew that I didn't really know what I was doing. My only hope was that this was a way out.

When I reached the ship, I waded around, trying to figure out what to do next. I didn't have to wait long though. Someone from above called to me.

"You there, don't move!"

A man leaned over the side of the ship and pointed a pistol at me. He tossed me a rope and ordered me to climb aboard. Upon reaching the main deck, I was commanded to stand still.

While I waited, I spotted Captain Hurricane's ship. It was fleeing. From this distance it appeared pretty damaged. There were a few holes in the side and plenty of debris floating on the water. I stared at it in silence, watching until it became nothing more than a speck.

Someone then spoke, breaking my trance.

"Who are you?"

"My name is Marlin Peracue."

"Turn around and face me."

I twisted around and a shocked expression crossed my face. Was I seeing things? This could not be the captain.

"What's the matter, Mr. Peracue? Never seen a woman before."

"I'm sorry. I didn't mean…"

"Well, of course you didn't. Now look, lad! What were you doing on Captain Hurricane's ship?"

"I was kidnapped from my homeland, La Pearl, and taken aboard as their cabin boy."

"Really? I've heard of La Pearl. But I've never had the pleasure of going there. Would you like me to take you back?"

"Well, yes. But…"

"But?"

But I remembered what Captain Hurricane had done to me, and anger and the desire for revenge burned in my mind. I wanted to pay him back for what he had done. I wanted to track him down and blow his ship up. He deserved to die.

No, wait! I needed experience. If I could learn to be a good sailor, working my way up. I could earn a name for myself and then take my revenge.

"I… would like to travel."

"You want to travel? Don't you want to go home?"

She waited for an answer, but I didn't have a good one. It was true that I missed my grandpa, but I still wanted revenge.

"Tell you what, Mr. Peracue. I'll make you a proposition. I'll let you tag along with me, and my crew for a while before we take you back to La Pearl. But only if you wish to… If you choose to do so, I'll make you a cabin boy. Will you do this?"

"I'll do it."

"You agree to the terms then?"

13

"Yes."

"Well, then welcome aboard the Specter, Mr. Peracue. You will be our new cabin boy."

"Okay, so are you a pirate?"

"Goodness, no. I'm an adventurer. I seek the unknown. You can call me... Captain Hornet!" She took off her hat and made a short bow. A second later she straightened herself. "I want you to expand beyond a cabin boy. I suggest that you work your way up from the bottom." Gesturing to a man with her hat she said, "Duke, please show Mr. Peracue to his bunk."

Immediately Duke stepped forward. He was a tall, broad-shouldered man with dark eyes and a serious expression.

"Duke is my first mate."

With another gesture from Captain Hornet, Duke led me away. I followed him down below and was shown to my bunk.

"This is where you sleep. I suggest you better start working, if you want to move up in rank."

After he left, I was handed a mop by a crew member, and I started swabbing the main deck. It was the same kind of chore I had done on Captain Hurricane's ship. I pretty much just helped around where work was needed to be done. While doing so, I heard some of the crew talking.

"Rumor has it we're going to sail to Doom Island."

"No, not that island! No one has ever survived it, and ships have never returned."

I stopped working, and a chill ran down my back. Doom Island? So, that's where we're going. But why?

Chapter 3:
A Lesson

A few weeks went by after that, and I finally learned the names of the crew. There, of course, was Duke who was first mate, and Eli who kept watch in the crow's nest. Then there was Saber, the navigator; Latimore the Boatswain; and Powder, the master gunner. The rest of the 75 crew members were just good sailors. In fact, they were all decent men who respected Captain Hornet, but only three of the crew members were close to her. Duke, Saber, and Powder had started with the captain from the very beginning.

While I was reflecting, a shadow emerged. Gazing up I met Duke's dark eyes.

"Marlin, Captain Hornet wants to see you."

I stopped what I was doing and hurried to the captain's cabin. I opened the door, and there she was, sitting on a chair next to a polished desk. She had a parrot, sitting on her shoulder. It was a beautiful, green bird with bright, blue tail feathers. It wasn't very big, but it wasn't tiny either.

"You wanted to see me?" I said.

"Yes, I was wondering if you know how to swordfight?" She asked, facing me.

"Swordfight?"

"Yes, if ever the ship were to be attacked, sword fighting would be one of your defenses."

Captain Hornet stood up and approached. I couldn't keep my eyes off her bird while she did so. She knew I was watching it. I wasn't afraid, but that didn't mean that the bird wouldn't bite.

"You're not afraid of parrots," she said. "Are you, Mr. Peracue?"

"Well, I haven't been around birds much."

"This is Peter."

The bird's eyes moved from Captain Hornet to me. It was as if the bird understood what she had said. It was cool.

"He is a very intelligent bird... Now you never answered my question, Mr. Peracue. Can you swordfight?"

"No, Captain Hornet. I'm afraid not."

"Well, today will be your first lesson then."

"Today?"

"Yes, here," she said, handing me a sword.

For the next hour, she taught me the rules

about sword fighting. However, I couldn't swordfight. No, from that point on I had lessons for an hour every day. For me it was difficult, but I eventually caught on.

As time passed, I grasped clarity about Captain Hornet's personality that I never realized before. Although she seemed stern, it really was just for show. Hidden behind that facade was a truly caring individual. It was that same goodness that I felt when I first met her. That somehow she was upright despite the strict form she presented. And one day during practice, I decided to be bold.

"May I ask you something, Captain Hornet?"

"Yes, I suppose so."

"Why do you want to go to Doom Island?"

She stopped in her tracks, resting on her sword. "You mean, Muthrion?"

"Muthrion?"

"Also known as Doom Island." She squinted at me. "Because, Mr. Peracue, hidden somewhere on that island is The Moura Tree."

"What's The Moura Tree?"

"Well, legend says that it grants us our most desired wishes."

"You mean, anything we want?"

"Yes, but there's a catch to it. The tree only grants it to those of pure heart; otherwise a curse will be placed upon them."

"What's the curse?"

"Marlin, by now you've heard how ships go to the island but never return. Have you ever wondered why?"

My eyes grew wide.

"Only a part of my crew will join me on the island when the time comes. And I'm not going to force you to go either, but the choice must be yours. Do you understand?"

I nodded.

"Good. Now." She placed her sword back in its sheath. "I think you've had enough practice for today."

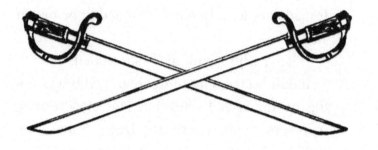

Chapter 4:
Doom Island

About two months passed, when Eli suddenly yelled down from the crow's nest. He spotted land in the distance. At last we had reached Doom Island. Soon after, we docked the ship off shore.

Captain Hornet stood on deck with Peter on her shoulder. The wind blew her hair around. It made her look fierce. I was glad to be on her side.

"Okay, who's with me?" she yelled.

It didn't take long to figure out who was going on the island with her. Her closest crew members stepped forward; Duke, Saber, and Powder. I then decided to follow them. I was curious about the island.

"Alright, Latimore, you are in charge while I'm gone," commanded Captain Hornet. "If we are not back in twelve days, I want you to take the ship and leave."

"Yes, Captain Hornet."

"Good, the rest of you give Latimore your full attention."

As for those of us going ashore, we were informed to bring weapons and provision. So, we quickly got rowboats and journeyed toward the island. When we landed, Captain Hornet commanded us to follow her every step and keep a sharp look out. It had been awhile since I'd been on land, and it took me some time to get adjusted.

We all then traveled up the beach, leaving imprints in the sand. Searching around we spotted a towering wall composed of rocks. The wall stretched all the way around the island. Behind it was an enormous jungle.

"I wonder how we enter?" asked Powder, the master gunner.

"Well, according to this map," answered Saber, the navigator. "We should find a stone entrance with a monkey face on it. It should be hidden around here somewhere."

"I didn't know you had a map to the island," I said.

"How else could we have found it, lad?" replied Duke.

"There it is!" said Captain Hornet, pointing to the monkey face. "What else does the map show?"

"The map shows that we're supposed to

walk through it and come out into the jungle on the other side."

"Well, then," said Powder. "What are we waiting for? Let's go!"

"No! Wait, Powder," said Captain Hornet, crossing his path. "I'll go first!"

She grabbed a torch, which was hanging on the stone entrance, and lit it. She led us through, and once inside we could see that it opened into a wide cave.

"Listen to me," said Captain Hornet. "Don't touch anything, not even the walls! This place is full of traps, so stay close."

Our footprints scrapped across the cold floor. Shortly after, we heard an odd clicking sound.

"Quick, drop to the ground!" ordered Captain Hornet.

We dove to the ground as a blaze shot out of the wall, barely missing us. After about a minute, the fire died down and stopped.

"Is everyone okay?" asked Captain Hornet, getting up. "Say Aye!"

"Aye!"

"Saber," said Captain Hornet. "Is there no way around this?"

Standing up, he studied the map for a moment under her torch. "According to this map, there should be a secret passageway just up ahead. We need to look on the right side of the wall for a monkey face just like the one on the entrance."

"Come on, mates, look for the symbol of a monkey face," instructed Captain Hornet.

We scanned the right wall for the symbol. There were engravings everywhere on the dusty, cold walls. It was hard to see in the dim light, but at last we found it. Captain Hornet then pushed against the monkey face, and the cave wall gave way, revealing an entrance. She beckoned us with her hand, and we trailed after her through a low opening. There was a narrow tunnel. We trekked through it and came out into the jungle. The captain paused in her tracks, snuffing out her torch.

"Why have we stopped?" I asked.

"Look," she motioned in front of her.

Right before us were gigantic, purple worms. At least that's what they looked like to me. They possessed two eyes and a mouth.

"What are those?" I asked.

"I don't know," answered Captain Hornet.

"But I wouldn't touch those unfortunate souls."

Suddenly, one cried out to us.

"Please, help me!"

"Everyone, back!" said the captain, pulling out her sword. "Quick! To the trees. It's our only way around them."

She pointed at the trees which were lined up side by side and connected to each other at the top. She put her sword in her sheath and clambered into a tree. Peter, her bird, clung to her shoulder as she did so. She gestured to us.

"Quickly, follow my lead!"

One by one the rest of us scrabbled into the enormous tree before the worms reached us. Luckily, for us, we were able to travel through the trees, so we could get to our destination. With each step, we gripped onto limbs, making sure we didn't stumble and plummet to the ground. Several hours later, the captain paused to make camp. So, we stayed the night in the trees.

All night long we could hear horrible noises that sounded like growling. It was an eerie feeling that kept me awake for a long time. Yet through exhaustion I finally fell asleep. However, it wasn't a peaceful sleep. I had horrific nightmares about dark shadows, and these shadows kept attacking me. I fought in my sleep until Duke woke me up the next day. It was almost dawn.

"Marlin, you need to get up. Captain Hornet says you need to eat breakfast."

"What?" I rubbed my eyes.

"We'll be moving soon."

I pulled out a crisp apple from the brown bag that I was carrying around my waist and ate it. After I finished it, we were on the move again. We journeyed through the trees for a few more hours until at last the jungle ended. Beyond it, was an enormous lake. In silence the captain crawled down from the tree to examine. When it was safe, she spoke.

"It seems to me that the only way cross the lake is by swimming. But since I don't trust the water, I propose another idea."

"And what's that?" asked Duke.

"We make a raft."

Therefore, we set to work, pulling out our hand axes. We started chopping down the trees around us. Hours later we had a sturdy raft large enough to hold us. Without wasting any more time, we set off on it.

Chapter 5:
The Lake...

We drifted across the water in silence. No noise could be heard, and there were no sounds of birds, crickets, or even frogs. The water was dark, green, and murky. Something didn't feel right as I gazed into it. Although I couldn't see into the water, I felt that something was peering at me from its depths. It was an uncanny feeling.

"Don't stare into the water," whispered Duke in my ear.

"Why?"

"You don't want to draw attention to yourself."

And nobody said anything else. We kept quiet until something stirred in the water. I leaned over the edge of the raft, hoping to catch a glimpse of whatever was down there. That's when something sprung out of it. The creature caught us by surprise, and we dropped down on the raft as a massive fish leaped over us. It landed back in the water on the other side. It was an ugly, green fish with bulgy eyes and a mouth full of sharp teeth. The fish's green coloring allowed it to blend in with the water, but it didn't take long for the fish to reappear. Once more it sprung at us. The difference was that this time the fish wasn't alone. Therc were at least six more with it.

"Look out!" said Duke.

I jerked out my sword to protect myself. But before I could do so, the fish exploded right in front of me. Its green scales and white flesh went flying. Baffled I turned to see Captain Hornet holding a pistol. Smoke was billowing out of its end. She gave me a half smile. I only caught a glimpse of it though. I had to arm myself against another fish. This time I was ready, and used my sword to slice the creature's head off. The decapitated fish landed back in the water with a plop. In a matter of seconds, all the bloodthirsty fish were killed.

"Is everyone okay?" asked Captain Hornet.

Sure enough, everyone was.

Chapter 6:
The Rock Land

The following morning, we landed on the other side of the lake. All night long we kept watch for more dangerous fish, but now the ride was over.

Stepping onto the land, it wasn't what I expected. It was nothing but rock. Yes, an enormous rock, and it went on for what seemed like miles and miles. There weren't any trees or grass. It was just a rock land. Still we set foot on it, the captain leading in front. While we shadowed her, she kicked a tiny pebble. The little stone fell into a small dent in the rock. When it did so, part of the rock, which was almost a foot in front of Captain Hornet, crumbled away into an enormous hole. In shock we all froze.

"It's the dents in the rock," said Duke. "We must be careful."

"Yes, so please watch me and follow my exact steps," instructed Captain Hornet. "There are little dents everywhere."

Without argument the rest of us trailed behind. We sure didn't want to step in the wrong

spot. But after a while of doing this, we became restless. It was hard to keep our minds
busy, but soon we reached the end of the rock.
And just beyond it, there was a yellow canyon.
The only way down it was a narrow, thin road,
but none of us felt like going anywhere. So,
we set up camp.

Chapter 7:
A New Friend

In the morning we trekked down the narrow trail into the canyon. The road was so thin that on the way down we had to keep our backs against the wall, so that we wouldn't fall off. Each and every one of us was connected to one long rope tied to our waists. If one of us fell, the rest of us could pull them up. It took us a few hours to go all the way down, but we made it. At the bottom of the canyon, there was a narrow stream. We followed the water to an entrance of what looked like an old mine in the side of the canyon.

"Shall we proceed?" asked Captain Hornet.

"No, there isn't a mine on the map," answered Saber, the navigator.

"There really isn't much of a choice though," said Captain Hornet.

After a moment, she lit a torch, and the rest of us went into the mine after her. Upon entering we spotted old mine carts in front of us. It was strange that there were all these carts, but nobody to work them. But we kept going until we had to stop at a broken, corroded track.

There was no way around it. A gaping hole stood between us and the other side. It was at least five feet apart.

"Come on, mates, we'll have to jump our way across!" said Captain Hornet.

She leaped first while the rest of us followed suit. Once on the other side, we continued to follow the remaining rusty rails. Nevertheless we failed to scout out the new area. So, it came as a surprise when an extraordinary creature popped out, blocking our path. It was an odd being that was about four foot tall. It had pointed ears and the face and body of a human. There were also bat-looking wings on its back. Other than that, it possessed bright, golden eyes and wore brown, ragged clothes.

"So, tell me why I should show you the way out of this place?" said the creature, eyeing us.

There was a lengthy pause after the creature asked this. We were all too startled to speak, except for Captain Hornet.

"Because if you show us the way out, we will give you something."

"What will you give me?"

"I don't have much to offer. But if you lead me and my crew out of here, I will give you as

43

much water and provision as you like."

Captain Hornet said this because she realized that the creature was starving to death. It was scrawny from lack of nourishment.

For a moment, it didn't look like the creature was going to give in, but finally it relented.

"Alright, it's a deal. But if you try to trick me in any way, I will bring you to a dead end and leave you there."

And with that threat, the creature led the way. The rest of us followed it at a safe distance. We were not sure what would happen.

"My name is Devlin," it said. "I suppose… You're wondering how this mine got here."

"Yes, we were wondering," answered Captain Hornet.

"Well, then I better start at the beginning."

Devlin enlightened us about the mine. He told us that all his friends and family used to work and live here until a terrible disease came and wiped them out. Now he was the only one left.

"When did this happen?" asked Captain Hornet.

"Several years ago…"

"Several years ago?"

"Yes. Now as part of our bargain, I have led you to the opening."

And he had.

"Thank you, and I promise that I will keep my end of the bargain."

Captain Hornet allowed him to search through our provisions to see what we had, and he grabbed what he wanted. Afterwards we hurried through the opening, which led into a forest. While we marched on, I glanced back at the creature. In doing so I noticed how pleased and sad he appeared to be. This long-ing that I felt coming from the being over-whelmed me.

"Would you like to come with us, Devlin?" I asked.

Everyone turned their eyes on me in amazement. They couldn't believe that I had just asked that. For one thing I wasn't the cap-tain.

"Me?"

"Yes, would you like to come with us?"

"You mean, you don't mind?"

"Nope."

"What about you?" he said, pointing at the

captain.

Captain Hornet squinted at me. I guess she was questioning my motives. She then peered at the creature. After a moment she answered.

"You may come with us, if you wish. But on one condition."

"What's that?"

"That you don't eat my bird, Peter."

Chapter 8:
The Guardians

Captain Hornet led us deep into a dark forest that lay before our eyes. It was huge with thick vines that wrapped around the trees. And enormous ferns covered the ground. There were massive plants with gaping, jagged mouths that would snap at us while we strolled by. And during all that time, Devlin circled us, using his bat wings. He chatted nonstop.

"So, where are you guys heading?"

"We are traveling to The Moura Tree," answered Captain Hornet.

"The Moura Tree? Then I guess you don't have much longer to travel."

"You mean, you know where it is?" I asked.

Yet before Devlin could answer, a shadowy figure popped out. From the waist up, it was human. But from the waist down, it had the body of a wolf. This creature was armed, carrying a spear. Several seconds later, more came out just like it. We jerked out our swords.

"Wait, put down your weapons!" said Devlin. "These are Faol (Phey-oil) Men. They are the guardians of the forest and of The Moura Tree which you seek."

"What do you propose we do?" asked Captain Hornet. Her eyebrows furrowing.

"Put down your weapons."

"But if we do that, they will surely kill us," said Duke.

"Not if you lower your weapons."

"Alright, you heard him!" shouted Captain Hornet.

Therefore we put our weapons away. The Faol Men glanced at each another. A second later they pointed their spears at us to follow them into the woods.

Over broken limbs and scraggly plants, we traveled long and hard into the forest. With every step, it seemed like the forest would grow darker, but we still followed them. After several minutes we reached their campsite and spotted the chief. He sat on a big rock that protruded upward from the ground, across the campfire. He stared at us with his yellow, glowing eyes.

"So, what brings you into my forest?" he asked.

"We have come seeking The Moura Tree,"

answered Captain Hornet.

"Many have tried to get their desires and have failed."

"We are determined not to fail," she answered.

"Yes, I can see that you have proven yourself worthy by coming here without attacking. So, I shall help you, but only if you give me something worthwhile in return."

Stumped, none of us spoke. There was nothing that we had that was worthwhile to the chief, at least that's what I thought. However, to my astonishment, Devlin revealed something from his pocket. It was a magnificent, blue gem, which was in the shape of a star. As he held it out, the gem sparkled. Devlin handed it to Captain Hornet, who gave it to the chief. The chief's eyes marveled at its beauty.

"Thank you, I will now help you reach The Moura Tree. But first come and rest."

"Rest?" questioned Captain Hornet.

"Yes, tomorrow I will have one of my trusted men lead you to the tree."

We were invited to sit around the campfire. The Faol Men gave us cooked fish to eat which was caught from the river that flowed into the forest. We were also given water to drink. The food tasted good. But I had something else on my mind. I wanted to know about the gem that Devlin gave to the chief.

"Why did you give the chief that gem?"

"So that you wouldn't die. After all, I've grown fond of you."

"But what kind of gem was that anyway?"

"A Blue Lumine. I found it in the mine."

"Is that what the mine was used for, to find gems?"

"Yes, there were thousands of them, and they all came in different shapes and sizes. And some of them held powers."

"What kind of powers?"

"Healing powers, like restoring health for small cuts and wounds."

"Wow, I'd like to have some of those."

"Yes, and some gems were used as weapons. If you threw them on the ground, they would explode."

"Did you use them much?"

"Only against dangerous predators."

"Does the Blue Lumine have any powers?"

"Only the power of beauty."

Chapter 9:
The Moura Tree

When dawn approached, the chief had a guide ready to lead us to The Moura Tree. He didn't talk much and only answered direct questions. I guess, he felt that it was his duty to show us the way to the tree, and we trailed after him in eagerness. Soon we would reach our goal, but that's when something unexpected happened. Without warning Captain Hornet collapsed. Everyone stopped short in their tacks, even the guide.

"Captain!" yelled Duke, running to her side.

"I didn't think it would be so soon," she said, sounding weak.

"What do you mean?" I asked.

"I didn't want to alarm you. But the truth is... I'm dying."

"What?"

"Yes, I'm afraid it's true. That's why I must reach The Moura Tree before the curse consumes me."

"I don't understand," I answered. "What curse?"

"My family curse. It started a long time ago.

When my great grandfather was alive, he was a ruthless pirate, who sailed the seas to plunder and seek gold."

"What happened?" I asked.

"He got himself into trouble by fighting a stranger from a distant land. Because of my great grandfather's rude behavior, the stranger put a curse on him, and anyone that was in his bloodline. My great grandfather died that very day because of the curse."

"What curse is that?" asked Duke.

"That my lifespan will only consist of thirty years."

"How do you know this?" asked Saber.

"Because no one in my family has ever lived past the age of thirty. That's why I must reach The Moura Tree before it's too late."

"When do you turn thirty?" asked Powder, the master gunner.

"Tomorrow," she said, closing her eyes.

"Come on, there isn't much time!" beckoned Duke.

"Wait!" said Captain Hornet. "Only one of us can go to The Moura Tree."

"What do you mean?" asked Duke.

"I understand now…"

"Understand what?" questioned Duke.

"That I'm not pure of heart. This whole time I've only been thinking of myself. I've been selfish."

"That's not true," answered Saber. "You're always looking out for us."

"No, I've put your lives in danger by coming here."

"But we wanted to come," I said.

"No, you don't…"

"She's right," interrupted Devlin.

The creature spoke up. He had been so quiet that I had forgotten that he was with us.

"If she reaches The Moura Tree with her desire, she shall surely die," he answered.

"Please," said Captain Hornet. "Let me talk to Marlin."

The others backed off, and I approached the captain. I felt shaky and confused. I had never seen her so weak before.

"Marlin, I cannot keep myself awake. I know it's selfish of me to ask. But you must try to do this for me. Deep down inside I know that your heart is pure. I trust you to save me."

Duke overheard her, and his jaw dropped. After all, he was Captain Hornet's first mate.

He was going to say something, but then Captain Hornet's eyes closed. And she fell into a deep sleep. I stood paralyzed. It was a numbing pain that I had never felt before. Duke, with the help of the others, then picked up the captain and marched on.

"Come on, we must hurry!" said Duke. "There isn't a moment to lose."

So, the Faol Man led the way again, traveling at a much faster pace. It didn't take him long to reach the area, and he soon stopped.

"Are we there?" I asked.

"Beyond those trees is The Moura Tree that you seek," answered the Faol Man.

He pointed to a cluster of trees ahead of him. He then took off and left us alone in the area. Shortly after, Duke turned to me.

"Marlin, the captain chose you to save her. She believes in you and so do I."

I couldn't say anything. I was still in shock. What if my heart wasn't pure? Gazing at Duke, I nodded.

"Don't worry," he said. "I know you can do it."

The rest of the crew nodded as well. I then hiked through the clustering trees alone and came into a clearing. There, in the center, stood The Moura Tree. It was a magnificent, knobby tree.

While I stood there, the tree wavered back and forth as though it understood my presence. I could hear it speaking. It was like its words were being carried by the wind.

"You come from far away, seeking a desire," it said. "But you must make a wish instead. And if you are not pure in heart, your wish will never come about. It will only be a desire. And then you will have no choice but to face judgment... Therefore, young one, come forth and state in your mind what it is that you truly wish."

Upon hearing those words, I comprehended what my fate could be. Yet somehow within me, I gathered up faith and courage. I stepped forward and knelt down before the massive tree. I closed my eyes. Within my heart I knew I cared for the captain. I truly had become fond of her. I pondered about how she always looked out for us, her crew, putting our lives before her own. But now it was she who needed saving.

It then occurred to me that I had been so

selfish in the past, desiring to leave home just because I craved excitement. If it wasn't for Captain Hornet, I would be dead. And that's when I realized that I didn't deserve anything. My heart sank. How could I be pure in heart when all I had thought about was getting my own selfish desires? No, I didn't deserve anything...

But Captain Hornet had changed me. I was no longer the same person who was kidnapped from home. I was no longer filled with hatred and the want for revenge for the suffering I received on Captain Hurricane's ship. No, I had transitioned. Compassion and kindness had been Captain Hornet's gifts to me, and now it was my turn to return the favor and save her. Removing all doubt from my mind, I believed in my wish.

I stood up, staring at the tree with unblinking eyes, suddenly realizing that I was crying, and for once I didn't feel shame as tears seeped down my face. The emotion within me was overwhelming, but it soon ceased. I then felt the most wonderful feeling that I had ever known. It was as if I had been enhanced by a great power. For a moment the world around me sparkled and then ended. When the sensation was gone, I continued to gaze at The Moura Tree.

"Mr. Peracue, what on earth are you doing?"

"Captain Hornet?" I said, turning around.

"Yes, it's me, Marlin. I knew that you could do it."

Her bird, Peter, was sitting on her shoulder as if it had known everything would be alright.

Chapter 10:
Home

It didn't take us too long to make it back to the ship safe and sound. The Faol Men led us through an underground tunnel. It was a shortcut to get us to the other side of the island quicker, and soon we were back on board the Specter.

"Captain?" said Latimore in surprise.

Latimore had taken charge of the Specter while we were on the Island.

"Yes, it's me, Latimore. You didn't take me for dead, did you?"

"No, Captain Hornet."

"Good, then make way to sail," she commanded. "And as for you, Mr. Peracue, I've been meaning to speak with you."

"You have?"

"Yes, it's about your home land, La Pearl. I made a bargain with you. Did I not?"

"Yes, Captain Hornet."

"Then I better keep my end of the deal. I know that you love being on my ship, but it's time for you to go back home. I'm honored that you sailed with us. I've even gotten the pleasure to know you. You saved my life, and I thank you for it. But now it's time for you to go back."

I knew she was right, and I was ready to go home. So Captain Hornet informed the rest of the crew that we were departing Doom Island and going to La Pearl. Months later I could see my homeland. I clambered into a rowboat, and Captain Hornet rowed me to shore.

"Mr. Peracue," said Captain Hornet.

"Yes, Captain Hornet."

"I would like you to know that if you ever wish to return to the sea when you are done with your responsibilities here, I will allow you to come aboard my ship again."

"Thank you, Captain Hornet."

I then scrambled out of the rowboat. While I was waving goodbye, I noted a familiar face on the beach. It was my grandfather. When he noticed me, he rushed over and seized me in his arms. He was so glad to see me alive, and together we watched the Specter sail off into the horizon.

Made in the USA
Columbia, SC
30 June 2020